OUR LITTLE ROMAN COUSIN OF LONG AGO

This edition published 2026
by Living Book Press
Copyright © Living Book Press, 2026

ISBN: 978-1-76183-151-5 (hardcover)
         978-1-76183-150-8 (softcover)

First published in 1913.

A catalogue record for this book is available from the National Library of Australia

OUR LITTLE ROMAN COUSIN OF LONG AGO

by

JULIA DARROW COWLES

LIVING BOOK PRESS

MARCUS

CONTENTS

CHAPTER I

GOING TO SCHOOL

"Come, Marcus; come Lucius; no more sleep this morning, or the cocks will be crowing before you are in school."

Marcus turned, and bounded quickly from his couch to the floor.

"I wish the cocks did not crow so early in the morning," yawned Lucius, sleepily.

"Come, come," said his mother, "a boy that is old enough to go to school, is old enough to waken early."

Lucius sat up quickly. The great regret of Lucius' life was that he had not been born on the same day as his brother Marcus, instead of six years afterward. Marcus could do so many fine things that he could not. But this year he had entered the school to which Marcus went, and he was very proud of the fact.

Slipping over the edge of the high couch upon which he had been sleeping, Lucius dropped to his feet with a thud. Marcus never used the stool—which stood beside each high Roman bed—and Lucius did not intend to either, now that he was big enough to go to school.

The two boys were quickly dressed, for they had only to slip into their tunics, which were like extra long sweaters without sleeves.

They were soon in the atrium, or main living-room, of the home. There they found Glaucon, the tall Greek slave who always accompanied them upon the street.

"Be sure, Marcus, to stop at the little bakeshop and buy some cakes for your breakfast," said Gaia, their mother, as they started off.

It was still dark, and the boys carried lanterns to light them along the way.

All up and down the streets of Rome, bobbing, sputtering little lights showed that many other boys were on their way to school.

"Good, here is Tullius!" cried Marcus, as he met, at a corner, the boy friend whom he liked best of all.

Behind Tullius was Aulus, the slave, or pedagogue, who always accompanied him upon the streets, as Glaucon did Marcus.

The three boys went on together and the two slaves followed. When they reached the bakeshop the boys bought a light breakfast, to eat at school.

Glaucon and Aulus were glad to be together. Although

slaves, they were both educated men who had once been free citizens of Greece.

After a battle with the Greeks, Glaucon and Aulus were taken captive and brought to Rome. There they were sold in the slave market of the city.

Gaius, the father of Marcus and Lucius, paid a large sum of money for Glaucon, for he learned that he was an educated man, and a man of good character. Quintus, the father of Tullius, bought Aulus for the same reason.

Every Roman boy of good birth had a special slave who went with him to and from school, and to all public places of the city. If well educated, this slave also helped him with his lessons outside of school. For this reason he was called the boy's pedagogue.

The pedagogue held a very important place in a Roman household. Marcus and Lucius were fond of Glaucon, and Tullius was fond, too, of Aulus.

As the boys hurried along the streets with their lanterns, Marcus saw a big notice posted upon the wall of a house.

He held up his lantern to read.

"It is a notice of the chariot races that are to be held in the Circus Maximus," he said. "There will be six drivers, and each will drive four horses. It will be a fine race."

Tullius was now reading the notice, too. "One of the

drivers has won more than two thousand victories!" he exclaimed. "My, what a lot!"

"I wish I could see a chariot race," said Lucius. "You have seen more than one, haven't you, Marcus?"

"Yes," answered Marcus, "and you will see one some of these days, too."

"We had better hurry on," cried Tullius suddenly, "or we shall be late for school."

"And the master may flog us," said Lucius.

"But, even at that," said Marcus laughingly, "we do not have so hard a master as the school boys of Falerii."

"Is it a story, Marcus? Oh, do tell it to us," begged Lucius, for Marcus was a famous story-teller among the boys.

"Well," said Marcus, as they started on, "there was a great battle many, many years ago between the Romans and the Etruscans. The Romans had taken many towns belonging to the Etruscans, but the town of Falerii stood upon a high cliff with great ravines on each side.

"Camillus was the general in charge of the Roman army. His soldiers had gone into camp and were wondering day after day how they ever were to conquer a city built upon such a site as that.

"But one morning, while the officers were planning and the soldiers were talking, they saw a strange company making its way down the cliff and straight to the door of Camillus' tent. The company was made up of a group of boys with one man apparently in charge of them.

"When Camillus came out to greet them, the man stated that he was a schoolmaster in Falerii, and that the boys were his pupils.

"'They are sons of the foremost men of the town,' he said, 'and I have come to deliver them into your hands. For you may be sure,' he added, 'that when their fathers learn what has become of these boys, they will surrender their city to you, rather than let their sons be carried away as slaves.'"

"Oh, what a horrible schoolmaster!" exclaimed Lucius.

"Yes," said Marcus, "he thought that he would be given a great prize for his act. But Camillus was a true Roman general, and he would not stoop to anything so low as that.

"'Here,' he cried, turning to a soldier who stood near, 'tie this traitor's hands behind his back, and give every boy a rod.' Then, turning to the frightened boys, he said, 'Take the rods and drive him back to your city, and tell your fathers that I do not fight with boys. If I cannot win bravely, I will not win at all.'

"The boys did as Camillus told them, and when the men of Falerii heard Camillus' message they said, 'We are willing to surrender to so just a man as that.' And they became subjects of Rome."

"That is a fine story, Marcus," said Tullius. "I wish I had as good a memory as you. But here we are at school, and just in time, at that."

CHAPTER II

LESSONS

"Are you sure my tablet and stylus are in the box, Glaucon?" asked Marcus, as they reached the school.

"Yes," answered Glaucon, "and your reckoning stones, too," and he handed to Marcus the box which he had been carrying.

Tullius took his box from Aulus, and the three boys entered the open building which was their school.

This building, which was called a pergula, had only a roof resting upon pillars, with no side walls. The boys had no books, for this was nearly two thousand years ago, and a printed book had never been seen.

"I understand that Faustus, who lives next door, has complained of the noise of our school, and says that we waken him too early in the morning," said Tullius to Marcus.

"If he would keep earlier hours at night, he would not mind wakening early in the morning," replied Marcus with a laugh.

"But cock-crowing *is* pretty early in the morning," exclaimed Lucius with a shake of his head, as he set down the lantern which he had carried and tried to make its sputtering wick burn more brightly.

"If we lived in a northern city," said the master, who had heard Lucius' remark, "we should not need to rise so early, for then we could play or work all through the day. But here in Rome, where it is so hot that every one must rest through the middle of the day, we should not have time to learn much if we did not get to school before daylight."

Marcus and Tullius, who were thirteen, took their places with the older boys. Lucius, who was only seven, sat with the beginners, for this was the age at which the boys of Rome entered school.

There were no desks in the room. The teacher, or master, sat in a chair upon a raised platform. Each of the boys had a bench, with a stool for his feet so that his knees could be used for a desk.

After all were in their places, the master left his chair and, going from one pupil to another, wrote a maxim at the top of each boy's tablet.

The tablet was not a block of paper, for no one had heard of paper in those days. It was very much like a slate, with a light wooden frame, but the part inside the frame was covered with smooth wax.

Writing was done by cutting letters in the wax surface with a stylus. The stylus was long and slender in shape, pointed at one end and flat at the other. The writing was done with the pointed end. When a mistake was made, or a lesson was to be erased, the wax was rubbed smooth with the flat end.

As they had no books, the boys studied both reading and writing from their tablets.

"Marcus, the son of Gaius, may read his maxim," called the master, when all the copies had been written.

Marcus arose and read, speaking distinctly and carefully.

"Very good," said the master. "Marcus will be able to speak before the Senate when he is a man."

Marcus flushed with pleasure, for no greater praise than this could be given him. He, like every Roman boy of good birth, hoped that some day he might occupy a seat in the Senate, and so he was careful to speak correctly and distinctly at all times.

After the reading lesson was finished, the pupils made many copies of the maxim upon their tablets. The form of the letters which these Roman boys used, so long ago, was the same as our English letters, but the language used was Latin.

Before the lessons in reading and writing were finished, the sun arose, and the sputtering lights of the lanterns were put out.

Then came recess, and the boys played games, and ate the breakfasts that they had brought with them.

After recess the pupils took their reckoning stones from their boxes, ready for the lesson in arithmetic. This was a hard study for a Roman boy, because of the Roman numbers which were used.

You will see some of the Roman numbers at the beginning of the chapters of this book, and you probably know that V means five, X means ten, L means fifty, and C means one hundred. In order to write the number one hundred and twenty-four, instead of writing 124, Marcus had to write CXXIV. Now, if you will try to subtract thirty-seven—which is XXXVII—from CXXIV, you will begin to see why Roman arithmetic was such a hard study.

The pupils began the study of arithmetic by using the reckoning stones. These were smooth stones which were counted up to the number given by the master. This number was then divided by separating the stones into groups; or it was added to by placing other stones with the number first given.

As the boys grew older, they learned to solve quite hard problems by mental arithmetic. They also had a curious way of using their fingers to help themselves when figuring.

"I am glad I do not have to study arithmetic with my fingers," said Lucius, on the way home from school. "I cannot understand that, at all. But it is great fun to count with the reckoning stones."

CHAPTER III

MARCUS' HOME

When Marcus came home from school, he did not toss his cap into a corner, and then have to hunt for it the next time he went out; but perhaps this was because he had no cap to toss. Roman boys always went bareheaded, although the sun was hot in Italy.

They generally wore shoes when upon the street, although their arms and legs were as bare as their heads.

The home of Gaius was a beautiful one, but from the street all the houses of Rome looked very much alike. The front doors all opened directly upon the street, and the yards or gardens were at the back of the houses, and were surrounded by high walls.

As Marcus and Lucius came in from school, they saw a very pretty sight. The atrium, or main living-room, was very large, and in the centre of the room there was a beautiful fountain. Beside this fountain sat their little sister Livia, playing with two of her favorite doves.

"How pretty she looks, Lucius!" said Marcus, and in a moment he had tossed her, doves and all, high in the air.

"Oh, I am so glad you are here!" cried Livia, hugging Marcus and Lucius in turn with her dimpled arms.

From the atrium, which was separated from the other rooms of the house only by pillars and curtains, the boys could look out into the garden. This also had a fountain, with graceful statues about it, and many sorts of beautiful flowers.

Gaia, their mother, was in the garden, and Lucius ran to her, picked a scarlet blossom on his way, and when she stooped to kiss him, tucked it lovingly in her hair.

"Where is Terentia?" asked Marcus, as he, too, came into the garden with Livia.

"I am coming," called Terentia, the sister who was between Marcus and Lucius in age. "Mother has been teaching me to spin the wool for weaving," she added, "and I have tried to make my thread as smooth and even as hers."

"And did you succeed?" asked Marcus.

"No, not yet," answered Terentia, "but I mean to keep on trying."

"That is the way to succeed," said a hearty voice behind them, and the children turned quickly, for it was the voice of Gaius, their father, who had come in unobserved.

"Isn't it almost time for dinner, Mother?" asked Lucius, looking at the shadow which the sun-dial cast, in the garden.

"Yes," said Gaia, "I think it will be ready very soon."

"That reminds me, children," said Gaius, "of a curious invention that I saw to-day in the home of Quintus. It was called a water-clock, and it marks the time, as the sun-dial does, but it is better, because the dial can only tell us the time when the sun is shining, while this water-clock tells the time on cloudy days, and also at night."

"What was it like, Father?" asked Marcus with interest.

"It consisted," replied Gaius, "of a vessel filled with water. A scale was marked upon the vessel, and the water dripped from a small opening, so that just a certain amount could escape each hour. The vessel is filled with water each morning, and by looking at the scale, at the level of the water, one can tell the hour of the day. Do you understand it, my son?"

"Yes," replied Marcus, "I think that I do. It seems quite simple, and yet it is curious, too. I must see it the next time I go to visit Tullius."

"I wish the slaves would hasten dinner," said Lucius impatiently, "for school makes me very hungry."

"You must learn to be patient, even though hungry," said Gaius, placing his hand upon Lucius' shoulder, "If you do not, you will never make a good Roman citizen or soldier. Do you remember the story of Mucius?"

"No, Father," said Lucius, who was always ready for a story. "Please tell it to us."

"Caius Mucius," Gaius began, "was a young Roman of noble birth. Lars Porsena, a powerful enemy of Rome, was camped with his army outside the walls of the city, and he had been there so long that the citizens had no food left. But, hungry and weak as they were, the Romans were not ready to surrender, so Caius Mucius made his way into the enemy's camp, determined to kill the king. However, by some strange mistake, he killed the king's secretary instead.

"He was captured and brought before Lars Porsena, who condemned him to be killed. Then Caius Mucius drew himself up and exclaimed, 'There are three hundred more Roman youths ready to do what I have tried to do and failed! And, to show you that we do not fear any punishment, or any pain that you may condemn us to, I will suffer my right hand to be burned in your presence.'

"With that he extended his hand and held it in the flame that was burning upon an altar in the king's tent. His brave countenance showed no sign of suffering as he continued to hold his hand in the flame.

"Then Lars Porsena exclaimed, 'If all Romans are as

brave as this, and can endure hardship without flinching, as this man can, I would rather have them for friends than for enemies.' And he straightway offered the city terms of peace.

"After that Caius Mucius was known as Scaevola, which means the left-handed."

"Ah, he was brave!" exclaimed Lucius. "And he saved Rome by it, too, didn't he?" And he continued to look thoughtful as they all went in to dinner.

CHAPTER IV

AT DINNER

The Romans did not use chairs when at the table, but reclined upon couches. They rested upon the left arm, leaving the right hand free.

As soon as Gaius and his family had taken their places about the table, one of the slaves removed their sandals, for a Roman would not think of eating in a private house with sandals upon his feet.

When the dinner had been served, Gaia, turning to Lucius, asked, "And what did you do in school to-day?"

"Oh," replied Lucius, "I had such a nice way of learning my letters. The master gave me a set of letters cut from ivory, and, after I had learned their names, I made words from them, by laying them on my tablet. I played that each ivory letter was a boy, and it was much easier to remember their names that way.

"The master praised Marcus, to-day," he added, turning to his father.

"What did he say?" asked Gaius, and Marcus answered

with a flush of pleasure, "I read my maxim so well, that he said I should some day be able to address the Senate."

"That is praise, indeed," said his father, and then he added, "I think you have your mother to thank for that. Ever since you learned to talk, she has been careful about your speech, and your mother uses the purest Latin."

Gaia flushed with pleasure at her husband's praise, while Marcus replied, "I know that that is true."

"I hope" Gaius continued, "that you will gain as much by Glaucon's teaching, for he is a good Greek scholar and can teach you to speak Greek language as well as you speak the Latin. We are fortunate in having such a pedagogue as Glaucon."

"Glaucon is teaching me to speak in Greek, too," said Lucius eagerly, "and he says that I do very well."

"That is good," said Gaia, smiling approvingly at her younger boy.

"Father," said Lucius after a pause, "one of the boys in school was flogged to-day."

"What had he done?" asked Gaius.

"He wanted to go to an exhibition at the circus, and so he took cumin to make him look pale."

"Aha," said Gaius; "and so the master saw through his trick?"

"Yes," replied Lucius, laughingly, "and he gave him an exhibition of flogging, instead."

"He was smarting from it afterward," added Marcus, "and Glaucon told him not to mind; that flogging was what made good men and women."

"Glaucon is probably right," said Gaius. "The rod is needed when boys and girls choose to be unruly."

"Father," said Terentia, speaking for the first time, "I hear that girls attend some of the schools."

"Yes," replied her father, "it is true, but I think no good will come of it. The daughter's place is in the home, and I believe it is better for her to be educated there. A girl should know how to read and write, and keep simple accounts, as you are learning to do; but the most important lessons for her to learn are how to care for a household, how to spin and weave, and above all, how to hold the love and honor of her family.

"I know that my ideas are beginning, in some places, to be looked upon as old-fashioned," added Gaius, "but they were held by our ancestors, and they lived worthy and honorable lives."

"We had a new fashion set us at school to-day," said Marcus with a laugh. "Titus, the son of Faustus, was brought to school in a litter carried by six slaves."

"I am afraid," said Gaius severely, "that Faustus will

some day be sorry for his foolish following of these new Greek fashions. Certainly Titus is able to walk, and need not be carried to school by slaves as though he were a great noble, or a lame old man. Children should be taught to be self-reliant, strong, useful, and honorable. Being carried about, needlessly, by slaves, does not teach them any of those things.

"My children," added Gaius, earnestly, "let us keep to the old Roman ideals, which make strong, manly men, and true, honorable women: let us avoid idleness and empty show, and foolish fashions, which will make us weak in body, and weak in character as well.

"I think you all know the story of Cincinnatus," Gaius continued, after a pause, "but it will do no harm for you to hear it again."

"No, indeed, Father," said Terentia. "We always love to listen to your stories."

"*I* don't remember about Cincinnatus," said Lucius. "Who was he?"

"His name was like your own," answered Gaius. "It was Lucius Quintus, but he was called Cincinnatus because of his crisply curling hair.

"He was a brave and noble man, and a good soldier, but he lived upon his farm outside the city, and tilled the ground with his own labor.

"At the time of my story, some of the people with whom the Romans had made a treaty of peace, had broken their treaty, and were going through the Roman provinces killing the people and burning their houses.

"The Romans reminded them of their promise of peace, but they would not listen, and they defeated the soldiers who were sent out against them, and kept them captive.

"Then the Romans saw that they must choose a very wise man as well as a good soldier, and must make him Dictator, and place him in charge of the entire army.

"They decided that Cincinnatus was the man who was needed, and messengers from the Senate were sent to bring him.

"They found Cincinnatus plowing in his field, but he wrapped his toga about him and listened with dignity to all that they had to say.

"He went with them at once to Rome, and took command. He ordered every Roman in the city who was old enough to enter the army, to be ready to go with him that night. Each one was to carry his arms, sufficient food to last five days, and twelve wooden stakes.

"No one understood what the stakes were for, but all were ready to obey his commands.

"That night, under his orders, they marched to the spot where the enemy's troops were encamped, and surrounded them. Then each man dug a trench before him and drove in his stakes; and when the enemy was aroused by the shout of the Romans, they found themselves surrounded and captured.

"Then Cincinnatus had two spears set upright in the ground, and a third fastened across their tops, and he made all the defeated army pass through, in sign that they placed themselves under the Roman yoke. After that he let them go to their homes.

"When Cincinnatus returned to Rome he was given every honor that could be shown to a victorious general, but a few days later he laid aside the office of Dictator, knowing that his work was done, and returned to his little farm.

"We need not all be farmers, as Cincinnatus was, but we should all imitate the simplicity and the dignity which made Cincinnatus one of the heroes of Rome.

"The Greeks, whose ways so many Romans are copying," Gaius added, as he finished his story, "have among them the best artists and poets in the world. I wish to give them all the credit possible for their art and their literature. It is only the idleness and the luxury of the Greeks that I am sorry to see the Romans imitating. It will not prove good for Rome."

CHAPTER V

THE VESTAL OFFERING

"Come, little sister, we must hurry, or we will be late at the altar, and you know Father does not allow that."

Terentia took Livia's hand and they ran together to the atrium.

Gaius and Gaia, Marcus and Lucius, and the household slaves, were all in the room, for it was the time of the early morning offering at the family altar.

The Romans did not know the one true God, but believed that there were many gods. They thought that one watched over the household; that another had charge of the fields, and another of the flocks; while still others protected the sailors at sea, and the soldiers in battle.

Vesta was called the goddess of the home, and in every Roman house there was an altar to Vesta at one end of the atrium.

When all the household was together, Gaius laid an offering of salt upon the altar, and prayed that the affairs of the home might be blessed. The ceremony was a very simple one, but it marked the beginning of each day in the Roman home.

"Oh, Mother," said Terentia, after her father and Marcus had gone, "am I to learn to weave to-day? I am so eager to begin."

"Yes," replied Gaia, "I shall begin to-day to teach you how to weave. You have learned to spin so well."

Gaia's loom stood in the atrium, and Terentia felt very proud and happy as she stood before it. Her mother showed her how to wind the wool upon the shuttle, and then how to thrust it back and forth through the warp of the loom. In a little while Terentia was able to manage the shuttle alone.

"Isn't it strange," she said to her mother, "how we can make just these woollen threads into cloth to wear! I shall try to make mine as smooth and even as possible, for then Father will praise me."

Gaia smiled as she said, "That is right, my daughter. It is only by trying that we can do good work, and your father will be pleased if your cloth is smooth and even."

Livia stood by and watched Terentia with a great deal of interest. The shuttle flew back and forth, back and forth, and the bit of cloth in the loom grew steadily.

"Mother," said Terentia, as she worked, "I heard you

say yesterday that our cousin, Cornelia, had been chosen to be a Vestal Virgin. Please tell me just what it means."

"I think you have seen the Temple of Vesta, near the Forum," Gaia said, "and, of course, you understand that the goddess, Vesta, cares for our homes. That is why there is an altar to Vesta in every house."

"Yes," replied Terentia, "I understand about that; but what do the Vestal Virgins do?"

"Inside the Temple of Vesta, there is, of course, an altar, and the fire upon this is kept burning day and night. It is never allowed to go out. The Vestal Virgins care for this fire, and although they have other duties connected with the service of the temple, this is their chief care.

"Those who are chosen, as our cousin Cornelia has been, are greatly honored, for no Roman girl can be called to a higher service. Cornelia is not yet ten years old. For the next ten years she will be learning the duties of the temple; after that she will care for the sacred fires upon the altar for ten years; and then for the ten years following she will teach those who have been newly chosen for the service."

"And must she leave her own home for all of that time?" asked Terentia.

"Yes," her mother replied, "she gives up everything else to serve the goddess Vesta. But it is so great an honor that very few of the Vestal Virgins ever return to their homes, even after their time of service is over.

"Your father was telling me yesterday of an interesting incident. A prisoner was being hurried along the street, when he and his guard met one of the Vestal Virgins. The prisoner dropped to his knees, and the Vestal Virgin granted him pardon."

"Can the Vestal Virgins do that?" cried Terentia. "How happy the poor man must have been."

Terentia worked thoughtfully for some time, and then her glance fell upon Livia, who had grown tired of watching the busy shuttle, and was now playing with her beloved clay dolly.

Presently Terentia turned to her mother and said, "Oh, Mother, may I have this first piece of cloth to use as I like?"

"Perhaps," her mother answered with a smile. "What would you choose to make from it?"

"Oh, a dear little tunic for Livia," said Terentia eagerly.

"That will be very nice indeed," Gaia answered. "I could not ask you to put it to better use."

It took many, many days of weaving before the piece of cloth was long enough for even the little tunic, for sometimes there were mistakes which had to be undone.

But at last the soft woollen cloth was taken from the loom, and Terentia looked at its pretty folds and held it almost lovingly.

"I can hardly believe that I made it," she said with a happy laugh.

CHAPTER VI

A ROMAN GIRL

The little tunic was very simply made, but it was new work to Terentia.

"Are you sure it will be nice enough for Livia to wear?" Terentia asked her mother, anxiously.

"Yes," replied Gaia, "I am sure it will be if you make it as carefully as you wove the cloth."

"What makes you smile at me so often?" questioned Livia, looking up from her favorite clay dolly, which she was drawing about the room in its little cart.

"Oh, by and by I shall have a surprise for you," said Terentia, "but you must wait and ask no questions."

Livia looked as though she would like to ask a great many, but she said no more.

Presently she asked, "Mother, may I go into the garden to play?" And Gaia answered, "Yes, and Terentia has sewed long enough now. She may go with you."

The children loved to be in the garden with its beautiful flowers and its sparkling fountain.

"Let us play with the ball," said Livia, and then she added, "Oh, here comes Lucius. Perhaps he will play, too."

After a while Livia grew tired of running after the ball which her little hands found it hard to hold, so she sat down by the edge of the fountain and called her doves, who came and perched upon her shoulder.

"Oh, see," laughed Livia. "The dove is trying to eat the beads of my necklace."

"There, there, naughty dove," said Terentia, "those are not good to eat. They are to keep the evil eye away from our little Livia."

The necklace, at which the dove kept pecking, was made from odd and beautiful beads. Some were in the shape of coins, some were tiny images, others were shaped like axes and swords, while the most beautiful were in the form of half-moons, or of flowers. These quaint little objects were made from many kinds of metal and stone, and they were strung and worn as a necklace.

The beads had been given to Livia when she was eight days old. At that time she had been named, a sacrifice had been offered to the gods, and there had been great rejoicing and merry-making.

While she was a baby, the little objects had pleased her by their bright colors and by the noise they made when jingled together. Now that she was older, she still wore them, as they were looked upon as a charm which kept the evil eye of the gods from her.

A little later Gaia came into the garden, and Livia soon climbed upon her lap.

"I wish you would tell us a story, Mother," said Terentia.

Gaia thought for a moment and then she said, "Your father has told you the story of Scaevola, the Left-Handed, and it has reminded me of another story connected with Lars Porsena; but this one is about a girl.

"Do you remember the statue of a girl, mounted upon a horse, that stands at the top of the Sacred Way?"

"Yes," replied Terentia, "and her name is Cloelia, but I do not know the story about her."

"Cloelia," said Gaia, "had been taken from home, with many other girls and boys, by Lars Porsena. He had been fighting against the Romans, and had defeated them. Then he had made some of the noblest of the Romans give up their sons and daughters as hostages of war, before he would take his soldiers away from their city. He thought that if he took these boys and girls away with his army, the Romans would not dare to offend him, for fear that he might be cruel to their children.

"Lars Porsena went into camp some distance from Rome, on the opposite side of the river Tiber. Then it was that Cloelia formed a daring plan. She, and several of her companions who were strong and brave, swam across the river at night, and made their way back to Rome on foot. The current of the river is swift, and it required great endurance to carry out their plan, but they reached Rome safely.

"However, the brave girl and her companions were to meet with a bitter disappointment, for the Romans decided that, although they admired the courage which they had shown, they must be sent back to Lars Porsena's camp, for they had agreed with the king that he should have these boys and girls as hostages of war, if he would take his army away from Rome."

"Oh, what a pity!" exclaimed Terentia.

"It did, indeed, seem so," said Gaia, "but the Romans knew that it would not be honorable to keep them, and so they were taken back to Lars Porsena's camp.

"But our story turns out well, after all," she added, "for when Lars Porsena saw how just and honorable the Romans were, and how courageous Cloelia and her companions had proved themselves, he called before him all the Romans that he had taken as hostages. Then he told Cloelia that she might choose one-half of their number, and he would send them back to Rome, free.

"Cloelia was as wise as she was brave, and she chose

the younger half of the Romans, and they returned to the city with great honor.

"At the close of the war, the statue which you have seen in the Sacred Way, was erected in memory of Cloelia's brave deed."

"That is a splendid story, Mother," said Terentia. "I am glad that there are brave Roman girls, as well as brave Roman boys."

"Come here, Livia," called Terentia later that afternoon, and when Livia came she slipped off the little tunic which Livia had been wearing, and put on, instead, the new one which she had just finished.

"It is for you, little sister," she said happily. "I made it all myself, from the soft, white wool of the sheep."

Livia hugged Terentia, and then danced about to express her delight, and when her father returned to the house she ran to him and showing him the soft, new garment, she exclaimed, "Terentia made it for me; every bit herself!"

Gaius smiled and praised Terentia, till she blushed with happiness.

"You will be a Roman matron like your mother one of these days," he said. And Terentia felt that he could give her no greater praise than that.

CHAPTER VII

THE FUNERAL PROCESSION

"The funeral of the general, Antonius, takes place to-morrow, Marcus," said Tullius, as the two boys were walking home from school. "There will be a great procession; suppose we watch it together."

"Call for me in the morning and I will be ready," said Marcus, as they parted at a corner of the street.

The funeral occurred very early. A public crier first went about the streets of the city calling aloud in these words: "The general, Antonius, has been surrendered to death. For those who find it convenient, it is now time to attend the funeral. He is being brought from his house."

Tullius, followed by Aulus, was quickly joined by Marcus and Glaucon, and they took their places beside the roadway.

"We shall not have long to wait," said Marcus, as they heard the strains of music in the distance, and soon the procession came in sight.

First there was a band of men playing upon musical

instruments, and following the band came a company of singers. The songs which the latter sang had been written in praise of the dead general, telling of his brave deeds in battle.

Next, strange as the custom now seems, came a group of men who were hired to laugh and jest, and make merry speeches to those who stood by.

"Now, look," cried Tullius to Marcus; "here begins the fine part of the procession: here come the ancestors of the general."

Now, in order to understand Tullius' remark, we must know that whenever a man who had done his country a public service died, a wax mask of his face was made, and this was very carefully kept by his family. It was placed in a cabinet made especially for it, with a written record of all his public deeds. For hundreds of years this custom had been kept up, so that some families had a very large number of these cabinets of ancestors. The greater number they had, the greater honor was given the family, because it showed that they came of a long line of men who had served their country honorably.

At the funeral of a great man, these wax masks were taken out of the cabinets and each one was worn by a man who dressed just as the one whose mask he wore had been in the habit of dressing on great occasions.

FOLLOWED BY THE FAMILY, THE SLAVES OF
HIS HOUSEHOLD, AND FRIENDS.

As these strange figures passed before Marcus and Tullius, the boys looked at them with the greatest interest. It was like seeing the great men of Rome for many centuries past, walking by in the order in which they had lived and served their country. As the figures passed, Glaucon and Aulus told the boys many interesting stories about the different men who were thus pictured; of the battles in which they had fought, or of the public cause for which they had stood.

It was like a picture lesson in Roman history. When the last figure passed, Marcus exclaimed, "I know better, now, what Father meant when he said I could learn a great deal from the procession, if I thought of what I saw."

"Now see!" cried Glaucon. "You know the general came home in great triumph from the war, a few years ago. Here we have a picture of his entry into Rome."

The boys looked eagerly. Before them pranced beautiful horses, followed by chariots of war, heaped with the richest treasures.

After the chariots came a long line of slaves to represent the captives that had been taken in battle.

Glaucon and Aulus looked grave as they watched these slaves file past, for in just such fashion they had been brought captive to Rome.

After the slaves, came the body of the general, carried

upon a high couch, and followed by the family, the slaves of his household, and friends.

Last of all came the torch-bearers, with flaming torches, even though it was day.

When the procession had passed, the boys turned toward the Forum, where a speech in honor of the general was to be given by Quintus, the father of Tullius.

CHAPTER VIII

THE GIFT OF A BOOK

There were no book stores in Rome two thousand years ago. There had been but few books made, and each one of these had been written by hand for some special person. The writing was done upon sheets of papyrus which were rolled into the form of a scroll. A book written in this way was not only highly valued, but it made an expensive gift.

"I have received many favors from the Consul, Crassus," Gaius said one day at dinner, "and I should like to prove to him that I am grateful for them." Then turning to Gaia, he added, "I think I will have a copy made of the book of Greek poems which was recently sent to you."

"It would make a beautiful gift, I am sure," said Gaia.

"I shall want the best sheets of papyrus that can be found in Rome," Gaius continued. "I think it will be well for Glaucon to go to the shop and select them. Would you boys like to go with him?"

"Yes, indeed," replied Marcus and Lucius.

"How is papyrus made, Glaucon, and what is it made from?" asked Lucius, as they were preparing to go to the shop.

"Papyrus," replied Glaucon, "is a reed which grows sometimes twice as high as a man's head. The stem is not round, but has three sides, and it is four or five inches thick. The outer covering of the stem is dark, but the inner part, or pith, from which the sheets of papyrus are made, is white.

"When I was in Egypt," Glaucon continued, "I visited a very large papyrus factory, and it was interesting to see how the sheets were prepared."

"Do tell us about it," said Marcus.

The boys knew that Glaucon had travelled in other countries besides Greece, before he had been taken captive and made a slave.

"The factory," responded Glaucon, "was in a large building with open courts. Tanks of water stood in each court, and great bundles of papyrus stems lay beside them. The stems were first dipped in the water to soften them, then they were taken inside the building, where the dark outer covering was peeled off. After that the white pith was cut into very thin strips with a sharp knife.

"When these strips had been dried," Glaucon continued, "they were laid upon tables, side by side, and other strips were laid side by side across them, and pasted down. This made them into large sheets. After being pasted the sheets were pressed, bleached to make them very white, and trimmed to the same size."

"Where does the papyrus grow?" asked Lucius.

"In Egypt," replied Glaucon, "and the largest factories are in that country."

Gaius was pleased with the fine, smooth sheets that Glaucon brought with him from the shop. He called for the slave who did his writing, and who, like Glaucon, was an educated Greek. This slave's name was Drusus.

To Drusus he gave the sheets of papyrus and the book of Greek poems. "I want an exact copy made," he said, "for it is to be a gift to the Consul."

Drusus was well pleased with the task, and went about the work at once. Terentia and even little Livia, as well as Marcus and Lucius, stood by while Drusus sharpened the reed pens and split their points carefully. He then filled the inkstands, one with black ink, the other with red, after which he took Gala's book from its case and carefully unrolled the first page. The headings and ornaments at the beginning of the book were made with red ink, and the writing which followed was done with black.

"How queer the Greek letters look," said Terentia.

"They are not at all like the Latin letters. Can you name any of them, Marcus?"

"I know the names of only a few," replied Marcus, "but next year, when I enter the grammar school, I shall learn to read and write Greek. I think that will be fine."

"I am learning to speak Greek from mother," said Terentia, "but I do not want to learn to write such queer letters."

One after another Drusus unrolled the pages of the book, and copied them upon the fine sheets of papyrus. The work went on rather slowly, for he took care to form each letter perfectly, so that the book should be as beautiful as possible.

After many days the last page was copied, the ornaments at the end were carefully made in red ink, and the writing was completed.

"Come, Terentia," called Marcus, who was watching Drusus at the time, "you will want to see the book put together."

Very carefully Drusus laid the pages side by side, lapped the edges one over the other, and pasted the many sheets of papyrus into one long strip. Then he added light wooden rods to the ends of the strip, and the book was ready to be rolled and placed in the case which had been made to hold it.

It had taken a long time to complete the work, but when Gaius examined it and saw how clearly and perfectly the letters had been formed, and how carefully the ornaments and headings had been made, he was very much pleased.

"It is quite as beautiful as my own book," declared Gaia, and Gaius added, "I think that it surely will please the Consul."

CHAPTER IX

IN THE SENATE

The lessons which a Roman boy learned in school were only a part of his education. Every boy was trained to be a soldier, and much about the government and the politics of Rome was learned by listening to speeches in the Forum. Sons of the Senators were frequently taken to the Senate, that they might listen to the best speakers and orators of the time. This formed an important part of the education of the Roman boy of good birth.

Marcus was not surprised, therefore, when his father said to him one morning at breakfast, "I want you to go with me to the Senate to-day. These are troubled times for Rome, and there are likely to be important speeches by the Senators."

Marcus was ready promptly. He liked to go to the Forum, which was the busiest place in all the great city, and they must pass through the Forum to reach the Senate.

The Forum was a large, open building with beautiful

carvings and statues, and it was between two of the seven hills upon which Rome was built. The men of the city gathered there every day to learn the latest news from the war, to listen to political speeches, or to attend to any public business, and it was always a bustling, noisy place.

"Has the army been defeated?" asked Marcus, as he and his father were on their way. "You spoke of trouble," he added.

"No," replied Gaius, "I fear that we have even greater trouble than that on hand. Some of the citizens are trying to stir up rebellion in Rome itself. Listen well to all that is said to-day."

At the entrance to the Senate they met Tullius, and the two boys, as sons of Senators, were allowed to enter the building. They took seats together, where they could hear all that was said.

Presently one of the Senators arose. "It is Cicero," said Tullius eagerly. "Now we shall hear him speak!" For Cicero was one of the greatest orators of Rome, and his writings and orations are studied in schools and colleges to-day.

It was very quiet in the Senate when Cicero began to speak, for all seemed to realize that he had important matters to bring before them. And they were not mistaken. He told them that there was treason in their midst: that traitors were seeking to destroy and betray their city and overthrow the government: and then, raising his right arm, he pointed to one of the Senators named Catiline, and exclaimed, "In the name of the gods, Catiline, how long will you abuse our patience?"

There was a great outcry at this, for Catiline tried to defend himself, but Cicero had learned of his plot, and boldly told the assembled Senators that Catiline was a traitor.

Then there were shouts of "Enemy of Rome," and in the midst of the confusion Catiline left the room and hastened away from the city.

Marcus and Tullius were greatly excited over all this uproar in the usually dignified Senate, and on their way home they denounced Catiline as fiercely, if not as eloquently, as Cicero had done.

That afternoon a group of boys gathered in the garden of Marcus' home. They were all excited over the wars, which were being carried on in the country between the Roman army and the army of an Eastern king. Now they were more than ever excited over Cicero's speech against Catiline.

"I wish I were old enough to fight for Rome," exclaimed Marcus.

"So do I!" shouted the other boys in chorus.

"Since we are not, suppose you whet our appetites, Marcus, by telling us some of your famous war stories," suggested Tullius.

"Yes, yes," echoed the boys. "Tell us some stories, Marcus." And, after a moment, Marcus began:

"About two hundred years ago, Rome had her first battle with Carthage, you will remember. At that time Carthage ruled nearly all the cities that surrounded the Mediterranean Sea, and so the people of Carthage said proudly, 'The Mediterranean is only a lake which belongs to Carthage. No one can so much as wash his hands in it unless he receives permission from us.'

"Of course when the Romans heard this they determined that the Mediterranean should belong to them, or, at least, that Carthage should be made to take back her boast, and war was declared between the two nations.

"I am not going to tell you the history of this war," Marcus continued, "but a story which is part of that history, and which shows the sort of stuff that Romans are made of.

"Rome had no naval fleet to speak of, and her soldiers would not have known how to manage a fleet if they had had one. But the people of Carthage had a big fleet of vessels, and knew how to handle them, too. Their vessels had sails, and besides the sails they had five banks, or rows, of oars, one bank above another, the whole length of the ship. The oars were moved together in perfect time by slaves, who had been trained for this purpose.

"But Roman soldiers are not to be discouraged," said Marcus proudly, "and since they knew that they must fight some of their battles on the water, they began studying how they were to do it.

"The gods always favor the brave, and one day a disabled ship floated ashore close to the Roman camp. Then the army went to work. They studied the ship to see how it was built. They cut down trees in the forest and hewed them into timbers and planks. And that they might have men to manage the ships when they were ready, they set soldiers in banks upon the hillside, who practised the motion of rowing with even strokes.

"At the end of sixty days," declared Marcus, "the Romans had a fleet of vessels ready to sail, and men trained to row them. That was the beginning of the Roman navy, which is now the finest in the world."

"Good, good," cried the boys, when Marcus had finished his spirited story. Marcus flushed with pleasure, and when he looked up, his father stood beside him.

"I am glad to see you boys so well occupied," said Gaius. "And I have some good news to tell you. Word has just been received that our army is victorious, and that the king who has fought against us for so long is dead. Now, indeed, Rome may rejoice."

The boys jumped to their feet and shouted lustily.

"I suppose Pompey will soon return," exclaimed Tullius eagerly, for Pompey was the general in charge of the army, and the return of a victorious general was one of the finest sights to be seen in Rome. It meant a magnificent procession, merry-making, feasting, and rejoicing.

"Good! Good!" exclaimed the boys again and then they scattered to spread the news.

But the boys of Rome were not to see Pompey's triumph quite so soon as they hoped.

CHAPTER X

ON THE FARM

School had closed, and Gaius had taken his family for the summer months to the large farm which he owned. The children were pleased at the change, and were interested in all the affairs of the farm, which was so different from their home in the city.

The farm was managed by a trusted slave, and the work was done by slaves, belonging to Gaius.

"It is like a farm, here, and like a city, too," said Lucius one day.

"Why do you think that?" asked his father.

"Because," replied Lucius, "there are olive orchards, and vineyards, and fields of grain; and there are presses for making oil from the olives, and wine from the grapes, and stones for grinding the grain. And that is all like a farm. But there are as many people here as in a small city, and there are great stores for all kinds of food, and there are big ovens for baking, like those in the city."

"Yes," said Marcus, "it is interesting to watch the men

at work, too. Some of the slaves are tool makers, and make the tools that are used for building the houses and sheds, and those for taking care of the grain."

"I like best to watch the sheep, and to see them sheared," said Terentia, "though the poor things look so strange when their heavy fleece is off.

"But it is fine then to see how the wool is washed and made ready to be carded and spun and woven into cloth, as we spin and weave it at home," she added.

"I like to see the bees," exclaimed Livia, "because I know that they make the nice honey for my bread."

"You must be careful not to be upon too friendly terms with the bees," said Gaius, "or they may sting you."

"Yes," Livia answered. "Terentia told me about that, and I stand very still when I watch them."

"And do you like the bees better than the pretty doves, or the saucy chickens?" asked Terentia.

"I like the doves and the chickens," answered Livia, "but the bees make such good honey."

"The little ones all like sweets," said Gaius with a smile. "And what has interested you?" he asked, turning to Gaia.

"I think," replied Gaia, "that I have been most interested in the work of those who weave the baskets and who make the rope. Their work is so new and strange to me."

"A Roman farm, like ours," said Gaius, "is a complete community, as you children have discovered. If we were suddenly to be cut off from all other people and places, we could go right on living comfortably here, for we make our own tools and our own buildings, and we produce all that we really need to eat and to wear."

The tools that were used on a Roman farm would seem very few and very simple to a modern farmer, even though so many kinds of work were carried on. Nearly all the labor was performed by the slaves, by hand, although oxen were used to draw the plow and to turn the stones for grinding grain.

There were large numbers of cattle on Gaius' farm, and some of the milk was used for making cheese, but Marcus and Terentia never had tasted butter, for no one knew how to make it in those days. Olive oil was used in its place, and large groves of olive trees were grown on every farm.

No one ever had heard of sugar at that time, either. Honey was the only sweetening known. But aside from butter and sugar, Marcus and his brother and sisters ate very much the same kinds of food that we have to-day.

Each day the children found something new to watch on the farm. One day the boys stood by the stone quarry and saw the slaves quarry stone and shape it for building.

At another time they watched them hew down trees, and make them into rough lumber, and on still another day they were on hand to see them sift great quantities of sand for cement, for a great many of the Roman buildings were made of cement. It was convenient to have all these materials on the farm, for new buildings were often needed for storing grain, or for sheltering the great number of slaves.

Several festivals and holidays took place while the children were on the farm.

"To-morrow," said Gaius one morning, "we celebrate the Ambarvalia."

The children knew that in the country this was the most important religious festival of the year, and they were eager for the next day to come. They would walk in procession, and carry great sheaves of flowers in their arms, and what could be more delightful than that? No work would be done by the family or by any of the slaves, and after the ceremony the day would be a holiday for all.

Early in the morning the slaves were brought together, and a very large company they made. The children looked at them in surprise, for although Lucius had said there were as many people on the farm as in a small city, they had seen the slaves only as they were scattered here and there at their work. Now it seemed to them that they formed a small army, as they were brought together for the celebration of the Ambarvalia.

Gaius, with Marcus and the other members of his family, headed the solemn and reverent procession. They were followed by the overseer and the members of his family, and all the slaves of lesser importance.

They bore great sheaves of flowers in their arms, and Gaius carried purifying water, while Marcus waved fragrant incense.

Young animals from the best of the farm's flocks had been chosen for a sacrifice to the gods of the fields, and these animals had been gaily decorated and were led in the procession.

All about the fields the procession moved slowly, even Livia holding fast to her mother's hand, and stepping gravely beside her. She understood what it was all intended to mean, for Gala had told her that they wanted to thank the gods who watched over the fields, for all the good things which the earth gave them, and to ask that the fields might continue to give them abundant harvests.

Marcus, too, had been taught by his father what the sacrifice meant, and how all the ceremony was to be carried on, for some day, when he was a man, he would take the place that his father did to-day, and offer the sacrifices himself.

After the fragrant incense had been waved, the sacrifices had been made, and the purifying water had been sprinkled, the ceremony was finished, and then they all walked reverently back to the house.

After that the day was given up to rest or to merrymaking, for the slaves were free to do as they liked, and so the holiday of the Ambarvalia was enjoyed by all.

"I suppose we shall soon be going back to Rome," said Marcus one morning to his father.

"Yes, my son," replied Gaius. "I am planning to send a letter to the city to-morrow, so that everything may be ready for us at home. We shall return very soon."

Glaucon, Drusus, and a few of the household slaves had gone with the family to the farm, and Gaius now sent for Drusus to write the letter for him.

"May I watch Drusus write the letter, Father?" asked Lucius.

"Certainly," replied Gaius.

Drusus first took two tablets such as Marcus and Lucius used in school, but each of these tablets had only one waxed surface. He fastened the two together by lacing cords through holes in one edge of each frame, so that the two waxed surfaces were inside. Then Drusus took his stylus and wrote the letter as Gaius told him. After it was finished, he bound the double tablet about with a cord, so that nothing could mar the inner surfaces upon which the letter was written. He then fastened the ends of the cord with wax, which he stamped with Gaius' seal.

The next morning a foot-runner was called and the letter was given to him to take to Rome.

CHAPTER XI

THE RETURN TO ROME

"The farm is nice, but it will seem good to be at home again," said Terentia to her mother, as they entered the carriage which stood waiting.

It would take two days to make the journey back to the city, and they were to stop over night at the home of Perseus, a friend of Gaius, as they had done on their way to the farm.

Perseus, with his family, always stayed at the home of Gaius when in Rome, and the exchange of visits was enjoyed by all.

The children were quite excited at the novelty of the journey. Gaius and Marcus were to ride on horseback. Lucius was to ride in the carriage with his mother and sisters, but he wished with all his heart that he were old enough to mount a horse and ride beside his father and Marcus.

The carriage had no seats, but was supplied with many soft pillows upon which they were to recline.

The family goods were made up into packs, which were carried on the backs of mules. Altogether, they formed quite a little caravan, and the children thought it almost as good as one of the gay processions of the city.

Lucius, who liked to "make believe," declared that his father was a great general returning from war. Marcus was his chief officer, the family slaves were those that had been captured by Gaius in a great battle, while the mules with their packs bore the spoils that had been taken—the gold and silver vessels, the rich silks and embroideries, and the massive armor of the conquered generals.

"And what are we?" asked Terentia laughing.

"We? Oh," added Lucius readily, "Mamma is a noble princess that Gaius, the general, met and married; you girls are her handmaidens, and I—oh," ended Lucius with a laugh, "I am her slave," and he flung his arms impetuously about her neck, while Gaia gathered him into her arms.

"Slaves don't do that!" said Terentia.

The road that they travelled that day was a quiet one. Now and then a foot-runner, or a messenger on horseback would meet them, or they would be passed by a two-wheeled cart with a high seat and a single horse to draw it.

After several hours of travelling, the children grew tired, and then Gaia read a story to them, and played games with them.

At noon it was like a delightful picnic, for then they all rested beside the road, while the slaves served the food which had been prepared at the farm.

Late in the afternoon, they passed one of the roadside inns or taverns, which had a sign in the form of a stork hanging before the door. In the doorway stood the keeper of the inn, who called lustily to Gaius to stop over night with him, and promised all sorts of comfortable beds and board, for a reasonable sum.

But Gaius paid no attention to the innkeeper, for the taverns of that day were used mostly by foot-runners and messengers, and they were neither comfortable nor clean.

The home of Perseus was but a little farther on, and at his door the family caravan halted.

Perseus bade them welcome, and in a little while the children of the two families were playing together about the beautiful fountain in the open court, and talking of games, and of school, which would so soon begin again.

Gaia and the wife of Perseus talked of household affairs, and of the life upon the farm; while Gaius and

Perseus discussed the recent wars, and the grave affairs of the state.

The home of Perseus was very large and very beautiful, but although he was a man of wealth and had many slaves, he chose to live outside the city, and to carry on his own farm.

Gaius and his family were so pleasantly entertained, that all were sorry when the time came for them to resume their journey the next day.

CHAPTER XII

ON THE APPIAN WAY

On the second day of their journey, the children had little time to grow tired or restless, for they had entered the Appian Way, which was always thronged with people, riding, walking, or being carried in litters.

This Appian Way was the main road leading to Rome, and it was the oldest, the best known, and the finest road in all the world.

"Notice, children, what a wonderfully fine road this is," said Gaia. "It was built by Appius Claudius for the Roman armies to march over."

The children looked at the road, which was of stone and very broad.

"I have heard father say," remarked Terentia, "that it is made from great blocks of stone, fitted so carefully together that it is not possible to tell where they are joined."

"That is true," said Gaia. "See, it looks like one great stone. It is a wonderful piece of work."

Just then the attention of all was drawn to a party of men on horseback. The men wore medals and badges, which showed that they had been honored by the government. The horses were richly decked, and their shoes, which were of leather, were tipped with silver, which glistened as they stepped.

"What beautiful horses," said Lucius. And then he added quickly, "Oh, see!" for following at a little distance from the horsemen came a two-wheeled cart, drawn by mules. It had an arched cover, to protect the occupants from sun or rain, and two ladies reclined within it upon a pile of gay cushions. The covering of the cart, the cushions within it, and the trappings of the mules were rich with embroidery, and were of the most costly fabrics.

"Who are they, Mother?" asked Terentia, as Gaia exchanged greetings with the ladies.

"They are the wives of the Consul, Crassus, and of the general, Galba," she replied.

A moment later there was a hurried clatter of hoofs on the road, and a government courier dashed by on horseback. He led a second horse.

"What man is that?" asked Marcus of his father, when he could speak above the din of the clattering hoofs.

"That is a government courier," replied Gaius. "He bears some government message, and he must ride with all haste. These couriers often cover one hundred miles in a day. That would be impossible," Gaius added, "if the roads about Rome were not so well made."

"Why does he lead the second horse?" asked Marcus.

"At the rate that he travels, he will soon tire the first horse. He will then jump upon the second horse, leaving the first to rest at some inn or government station."

Marcus turned to watch the dashing rider, but he was soon out of sight.

"Is there likely to be another war, Father?" asked Marcus. "I hear talk of it, when you and your friends are together."

"It is not certain yet," replied Gaius, "but it is likely. Rome has had many wars, and the Roman armies are well drilled, so that we may count upon success if this war is undertaken."

"I wish I were older," said Marcus.

"You will soon enter the grammar school," replied his father, "and then your training for war will begin. You will learn how to ride, run, box and swim, as every Roman boy does, for you must be ready to serve your country if there is a call to arms."

Marcus' eyes shone. He was eager to begin this training, as was every Roman boy.

"See, Mother," said Livia, "see all the carts loaded with vegetables."

"Yes," replied Gaia, "the drivers are taking them to the markets in Rome, so that we may have fresh vegetables to eat."

As the occupants of the carriage looked at the loaded carts, a litter was borne swiftly past them, carried by eight slaves who ran swiftly, keeping perfect step. The cover of the litter was richly carved, and the curtains were of beautifully embroidered fabrics.

In spite of all the interesting sights, Livia's head began to nod. But Gaia soon called to her, "Wake up, little girl, for we are close to the walls of Rome, and now you must walk. See, we shall soon be at home again."

Livia opened her eyes, for the carriage had stopped, and her father was ready to lift her out.

They were just outside the walls of Rome, and here they must dismount and walk to their home, for at that time no one was permitted to drive in the streets of the city.

Gaius' letter had been received, and everything was in readiness for them. As they reclined about the table a little later, Lucius said, "It is nice to go away, but I believe it is even nicer to be at home again." And all the family agreed that he was right.

CHAPTER XIII

MARCUS ENTERS GRAMMAR SCHOOL

After their return from the farm, Marcus, still attended by Glaucon, entered the grammar school.

This school was quite different from the elementary. The walls of the room were decorated with marble tablets; busts of authors were placed here and there; and lutes, to be used in studying music, were hung upon the walls.

When Marcus first entered this school, he looked about the beautiful room, and then at his book, the first one that he ever had owned. It was "The Odyssey," a poem of the Trojan War, written by the Greek poet, Homer. Marcus' heart filled with pride, and he determined to do his best to win the praise of his new master.

Because of Glaucon's careful teaching, Marcus could speak the Greek language well. But now he would learn to read and write it, also.

In Rome, every boy was expected to be ready for the duties of a soldier, so that he could serve his country well

in time of war. This was made a part of the training of
the grammar school.

Every day, Tullius and Marcus went together to the
Campus Martius, where they were given lessons in riding, wrestling, running, leaping, and boxing. They also
had lessons in swimming, for a Roman soldier never
knew when he might have to swim a stream that lay
across the army's line of march. The river Tiber, which
flows through Rome, bounded the Campus Martius on
two sides, and gave the boys a fine place for swimming.

The Campus itself was a large, level, open space
between the Tiber and two of the seven famous hills of
Rome. It was a fine place for all kinds of athletic exercises
and military drills, and it was called the playground of
Rome.

The schoolboys enjoyed this part of their military
training immensely, and groups of citizens often gathered
to watch them at their exercises.

"Oh, I wish I were old enough to drill as Marcus does,"
sighed Lucius one day.

"You will learn to be a soldier quite soon enough, my
son," said Gaia. "And, besides, you can begin even now
to practise being a soldier."

"How can I do that?" asked Lucius eagerly.

"By being brave, and manly, and obedient," said Gaia.

"A soldier, you know, obeys commands instantly. A very small boy can practise that."

"Yes," replied Lucius, "I will try to do that; but I wish I could ride, and swim, and run, and wrestle, too."

"Would you like to go to the Campus Martius, some day, and watch Marcus and Tullius at their exercises and athletic drills?" asked Gaius.

"Oh, yes, indeed, Father," cried Lucius eagerly.

"Very well," said Gaius, "I will take you with me to see them."

Lucius ran to tell Terentia, for this would be almost as nice as taking part in the exercises themselves.

"Oh, Marcus," he called, when Marcus came in to dinner, "Father has promised to take me to the Campus to watch you and Tullius drill."

"That will be fine," said Marcus, "but I hope my horse will not throw me when you are there, as he did to-day."

"Were you hurt?" asked Lucius. "How did it happen?"

"He had not been ridden for a day or two and was feeling pretty good, and I was perhaps a bit careless in handling the reins. No," Marcus added, answering the first question last, "I was not hurt, but I had a pretty good shaking, which I can feel in my bones yet."

"What did the riding master say?" asked Lucius, who was as full of questions as boys of his age usually are.

"Fortunately," replied Marcus with a laugh, "he did not see the tumble.

"I wonder if dinner is ready," he added. "My shaking up has given me an appetite."

"Father is not here, yet," said Lucius. "Won't you tell me a story while we wait for him?"

"I think," said Marcus, "that I have told you the story of Romulus, who founded Rome." "Yes," replied Lucius, "but I want to hear it again. I hope," he added, "that when I am older I can remember the Roman stories as well as you do."

"Then this is the first one for you to know," said Marcus, "so listen well, and I will tell it to you very briefly:

"Romulus and Remus were twin brothers who were born in Italy before there was any such city as Rome. But while they were little babies they were thrown into the river Tiber to be drowned, because the king of the country was afraid that when they grew up, they would take his throne from him. He knew that he had no right to the throne, and that the grandfather of these boys should have been king instead.

"But the boys, who were in a wooden cradle, floated ashore instead of drowning, and a she-wolf heard them crying. She went to them, and because the gods were protecting them, she nursed them instead of harming them.

"In this way the boys were kept alive until they were found by a shepherd, who took them home to his wife.

"When they had grown to be men, Romulus and Remus helped to restore the throne to their grandfather. They then determined to build a city upon the spot where they were saved from the Tiber, and so they founded the city of Rome. In order to decide which one the city was to be named after, the brothers each went to the top of a hill and waited for some sign from the gods. Remus saw a flight of six vultures, but Romulus saw a flight of twelve, so the city was named after Romulus, and called Rome."

"Ah, here comes father," exclaimed Lucius, as Marcus brought his story to an end. Then he added, "I shall surely try to remember that story."

CHAPTER XIV

THE FESTIVAL OF VIOLETS

The mild Italian winter passed, spring came, and with it the season of violets: beautiful fragrant violets which grow so freely in Italy.

"Come, little sister, to-day is the festival of violets," cried Terentia as she wakened Livia early one morning.

Livia opened her eyes. She did not know just what Terentia meant, but she thought it must be something nice, for she loved the violets, and besides, Terentia looked so eager and happy.

The girls were soon in the atrium, and there they found Gaia and her maidens busily at work making wreaths from the beautiful flowers.

Terentia was soon helping, and Livia, too, for she could hand the blossoms to her mother as she fashioned them into wreaths.

When Gaius came in, with Marcus and Lucius following, the morning offering was made to Vesta at the family altar, and immediately after breakfast the ceremonies of the festival began.

On one side of the atrium of Gaius' home were the cabinets of ancestors. These cabinets were of carved and polished wood, the doors of which were usually closed. But on the morning of the festival of violets they were opened, and the children stood before them with a feeling of reverence, mingled with curiosity.

The cabinets held the wax masks or images of Gaius' ancestors. Each mask was fitted over a carved bust, so that they were very much like the sculptured busts of great men that we see in the art stores of to-day, only that the mask of wax looked more lifelike than one of stone or clay.

The family stood before each cabinet as it was opened, and Gaius told them of the life and deeds of the man before them; of the debates that he had led in the Senate, or of the brave deeds that he had performed in battle.

Then one of the members of the family crowned the bust with a fragrant wreath of violets.

Many of Gaius' relatives and friends had been invited to the house. Each one was furnished with great bunches of flowers, and after the busts had been crowned with violets they all set out for the family tomb, which was outside the gates of the city, on the Appian Way.

The Romans had great reverence for their dead, but these festivals were looked upon as holidays and not as a time of mourning.

"Come, let us look inside," said Marcus to Terentia, when they had reached the tomb.

"It is beautiful," said Terentia, stepping in and looking about her.

The inner walls were tinted in soft colors, beautiful lamps were burning, and artistic vases were placed about. It looked like a quiet, stately room.

"See," said Marcus, "here are the weapons of the general, our uncle," and he bent to examine a richly wrought sword.

"And, look," added Terentia, "at the ornaments and combs and mirrors of his wife, our aunt.

"And, oh," she added, a moment later, "I suppose these belonged to their little girl," and she turned to a table upon which were arranged a doll, a string of beads similar to those Livia wore, and several toys.

Among the weapons, the ornaments, and the toys, Marcus and Terentia laid lovingly the bunches of fragrant violets which they carried. Wreaths had already been hung about the tomb by Gaius, Gaia and their friends, and offerings of food were placed upon a table.

"Come, children, the feast is ready," called Gaia.

Outside, the guests were seated upon the green grass, and Marcus and Terentia took their places near Gaia. Then all were served to a supper of bread and wine, vegetables and eggs.

"Have you had a nice time, Livia?" asked Terentia, as they walked home.

"Oh, yes," said Livia. "The violets are so sweet."

"I liked it better than the Ambarvalia at the farm," said Terentia.

"It is nice to have a feast like this," said Marcus, "but I like the Ambarvalia better, with its sacrifice of many animals."

"The feast days are all fine," said Terentia, "but I love the festival of violets best of all."

CHAPTER XV

MARCUS, THE TORCH-BEARER

"I have a bit of news for you, Marcus," said Gaia one day as Marcus came in from school. "Our cousin, Lucilla, has chosen you to be torch-bearer at her wedding."

"Oh," cried Marcus, "do you mean that I am to carry the white thorn torch?"

"Yes," replied Gaia. "That is what Lucilla wishes."

"There will be a great wedding, I suppose," said Marcus. "That will be fine."

As soon as he could find Tullius the next morning, Marcus told him the news.

"Oh, how good," said Tullius. "What fun we will have together, for I have been chosen to bear the basket of offerings for the altar."

"Good, indeed!" exclaimed Marcus. "The wedding is to be a grand one, and we will have a great feast, too."

The home of Lucilla's father was a beautiful one, and on the day of the wedding it was decorated with flowers, with branches of trees, and with woven hangings of rich colors.

Before sunrise the guests began to arrive.

Marcus and Lucius were standing beside one of the pillars of the atrium when the bride and groom entered.

After them came Tullius with his basket of offerings. These were laid upon the family altar. The bride and groom sat before it, and prayers were made to the Roman gods.

The ceremony was a very simple one, but the feast which followed it lasted for many hours. It was not until evening that the guests arose from their couches about the table.

Tullius turned to Marcus. "Now," he said, "it is your turn to take part in the ceremonies." A procession was formed by the guests to take the bride from her father's house to the house of the groom. First there were torch-bearers, and following these were flute players. Then, directly in front of the bride, came Marcus, bearing the wedding torch of flaming white thorn.

Lucius was sure that no one of all the guests was so honored as Marcus. He felt quite certain that he would rather be Marcus than the groom himself!

The procession was a merry one, and there was music and the sound of happy laughter. Crowds of citizens stood along the way, for the Romans loved a procession of any sort, and a wedding procession was the merriest of all.

When they reached the home of the groom, Lucilla wound bands of woollen cloth about the pillars of the doorway, and then the invited guests entered the new home.

A fire had been laid on the hearth, and Marcus handed the white thorn torch to Lucilla, who lighted the hearth fire with it. Then turning, she tossed it, still burning, among the guests.

There was a merry scramble to catch it, as there is to-day to catch a flower from the bride's bouquet.

"Ah," cried Tullius. "See! Terentia has caught the torch. 'Tis a sign that she will be the next bride."

There was a bright flush upon Tullius' cheeks as he spoke. To be sure Terentia was but thirteen years old, but most Roman girls were married at the age of fourteen.

CHAPTER XVI

THE CHARIOT RACE

"I saw the horses and the chariots that are to take part in the races," cried Marcus as he came in from school. "They were just coming through the gates, into the city, as I was on my way to the Campus."

Lucius' eyes shone. "Oh, I wish I had been there!" he exclaimed. "But what do you think? Father says we are all to go and see the races to-morrow."

"Did he?" said Marcus, and away he ran to see if Terentia had heard the good news.

The Roman races were held in the circus, which was a very large uncovered space, with rows of raised seats along the sides. The seats held many thousand people, for the Romans were very fond of sports which were dangerous and exciting.

When Gaius and his family took their places, the seats were already crowded, and for some time the children found plenty to interest them in the big assembly of people who were laughing, talking, and greeting friends.

After Gaius had spoken to friends who were near, he turned to the children. "You see the gates at the upper end of the circus," he said. "Those close the stalls where the horses and their drivers are waiting for the signal to begin the race.

"Notice, too," he said, "the pedestal near the stalls. There are seven balls upon its top. The chariots will be driven seven times around the course, and each time one ball will be taken from the pedestal."

Suddenly the talking and laughing stopped, for the signal for the race had been given.

The doors of the stalls flew open. Lucius' eyes shone, for this was the first chariot race he ever had seen. He looked eagerly at the gay trappings of the prancing horses, at the handsome chariots, and at the drivers standing erect and holding firmly the reins of the restless horses.

"How strangely the drivers are dressed," he said to Marcus, for he had noticed that each man wore a close fitting cap, that leather cords bound the short tunic about the body, and that the shoulders, hips, and legs were protected with heavy leather coverings.

"That is to keep them from being too badly hurt, if they should happen to be thrown from their chariots," said Marcus.

Lucius' eyes opened more widely still, but there was no time then for further questions, for, at that moment, the starting signal was given, and the chariots, each with its four horses abreast, began their wild race.

Many times it seemed as though the wheels of the chariots must lock, or crash together, as the horses plunged ahead, and each driver tried to secure the shortest turn.

"I hope the red will win," said Marcus, watching eagerly the four black horses which bore his favorite color.

Six balls had been taken from the pedestal, and the last lap of the race was being driven. The black horses were ahead; their driver was strong and daring, and with a cry of triumph, which was echoed by thousands of the people, he crossed the line. The red had won!

The other horses and chariots were driven into their stalls, but the victor, standing very erect, drove once more down the length of the circus. But he drove slowly this time, and as he passed, the people threw flowers and gifts into the chariot, until he reached the end of the course and passed out through the arch of triumph.

"That was a fine race," said Lucius, as the boys made their way through the throng. "I am glad none of the drivers were thrown out."

"Ho," scoffed a boy who was near them. "You are no

THE LAST LAP OF THE RACE WAS BEING DRIVEN.

true Roman. There should have been at least one chariot smashed to make it really exciting.

"Have you never seen a fight of gladiators?"

"No," answered Lucius, "not yet."

"Well," replied the boy, "after you have seen a fight between gladiators and wild beasts in the arena, you will think a chariot race like this a pretty tame affair."

CHAPTER XVII

THE VICTORIOUS GENERAL

There was excitement in the city of Rome. The Senate had decreed that Pompey was to be given a magnificent triumph. Though it was two years after his great victory which Gaius had announced to the boys, he was now about to return to the city.

It was hard for the boys of Rome to go to school during the days that followed, and harder still for them to give attention to their lessons. They listened to every noise outside, and when at last the messengers on horseback dashed into the city to announce Pompey's return, the whole populace of Rome poured into the streets, and school and all else was forgotten.

Such a triumphant procession had never before been seen by the boys. It was two days in entering the city.

Marcus and Tullius hastened early in the morning to the Arch of Triumph, through which a victorious general always passed into Rome.

"They are coming," shouted Marcus, for the noise

of trumpets, of tramping horses, and of clanking armor could already be heard. And as the long procession passed through the great arch and into the city's streets, the boys watched with increasing wonder and amazement.

First there came a throng of people from all parts of the known world, followed by wagons piled with all the trophies of war. Some of the wagons were filled full of gold coins, others were piled with silver, and still others held the armor of the defeated army.

"What are those?" questioned the boys, as still more wagons came into view, loaded with strange looking objects.

"Those," answered a soldier who was standing near, "are the beaks of ships which were captured and destroyed."

"My!" exclaimed Tullius, "there must have been a whole fleet captured. Look at the wagons still coming! What curious figures they had on their ships. I should like to see such a fleet on the water."

When the wagons had all passed, there followed troops of captives that Pompey had taken in his battles. Some of these were pirates, some were soldiers, some were sea-men, while among them were conquered generals and even kings, who walked among the captives in token of their submission to Rome.

There Followed Troops Of Captives That
Pompey Had Taken In His Battles.

"Look, look," exclaimed Marcus, when these had passed, for there now appeared a monstrous image of the conquered king, who had killed himself rather than surrender. The image was nearly twelve feet tall, and was made of solid gold.

Then came figures representing battle scenes, with images of the enemies that had been slain, and last of all, in a magnificent chariot studded with flashing jewels, and attended by his generals, came Pompey himself.

It took two days for all this procession to pass through the Arch of Triumph, but, tired as they were when the first night came, the boys were too excited to sleep long, and early on the second morning they ran to the Forum, in order that they might see the last sights of all this wonderful triumph.

"I suppose the captives will all be slain," said Marcus, as they reached the Forum. For even the boys of Rome were so accustomed to violence and bloodshed, that they thought but little of having hundreds of captives put to death.

"No," answered Tullius, "Father says that Pompey has given orders that, after the celebration, the captives shall be returned to their homes, but the kings will, of course, be put to death."

"Of course," assented Marcus. And then he added, "I am glad the others are to be sent back, instead. Father says Pompey has proved himself a wise general. My!" he added, "what loads and loads there were of gold and silver. He must have conquered a rich country, and it will add greatly to the strength and glory of Rome."

"Yes," added Tullius, "and did you notice the throne and couch of the conquered king? I am glad we have no king in Rome."

"So am I," said Marcus. "I am glad that the conspiracy of Catiline was discovered, and the traitors put to death."

The Forum was crowded with people, but the boys managed to find places where they could view all the sights of the great celebration. Glaucon and Aulus accompanied them, as usual.

"The place is so full of people that they even stand in the Curtian Lake," said Marcus with a laugh.

"What gave that little pool of water its name?" asked Tullius. "You know all the old Roman stories. Can you tell me that?"

"Why, yes, indeed," replied Marcus. "It was named after a Roman warrior, Marcus Curtius. A terrible chasm opened in the Forum at one time, and the Romans did their best to fill it with earth; but the earth disappeared as fast as it was thrown in. Then they appealed to the gods to help them, and the oracle said that the chasm would never close until the dearest thing in Rome was thrown into it. After that the city would be secure forever.

"Then Marcus Curtius came forward, dressed in rich

armor, and riding the horse which had carried him into many successful wars. 'The warriors of Rome are her dearest possession,' he exclaimed, 'and I offer myself as a sacrifice for the city.' With that he rode his horse into the chasm, and disappeared from sight.

"The chasm closed, and the little pool which was left to mark the spot has been called the Curtian Lake ever since."

"Ah, that was fine," cried Tullius. "Such stories make one proud to be a Roman!"

At last the great procession was ended; the two captive kings were put to death; sacrifices were offered to the gods, and the tired people of Rome returned to their homes.

"Was there ever so great a triumph in Rome before?" Marcus asked his father the next morning at breakfast.

"Only once," replied Gaius, "and that was when Scipio conquered Carthage. That triumph lasted three days. Instead of there being a golden image of the conquered king, the great King Perseus himself walked in the procession, dressed all in black, and his children were among the captives, while the quantity of golden treasure was almost as great."

"What wonderful conquests Rome has made!" exclaimed Marcus.

"Yes," said his father, "it well deserves its name of 'Capital of The World.'"

CHAPTER XVIII

MARCUS, THE MAN

Several years had passed, and Marcus was now seventeen years old. His birthday was always celebrated by the family, but never as it would be this year, for he had reached the age at which the boys of Rome put aside boyish affairs and became citizens of the Republic.

Marcus could hardly wait for the great day to come, for then he would put on, for the first time, the toga, the garment which only a citizen of Rome might wear: then he would take his place among the men of Rome.

Gaius sent invitations to all the relatives and friends, asking them to celebrate the feast with him, for he wanted Marcus to be shown as much honor as possible.

Very early in the morning the ceremonies began. After the company had gathered, Marcus took his place before the family altar, and laid upon it his boyhood emblems. For the first time since he was eight days old, he took from his neck the bulla, or locket of gold, which his father had placed there when he was named. This he laid upon the altar, and beside it he placed his white tunic, with its purple stripe, which showed him to be of noble birth; and Gaius then offered a sacrifice upon the altar.

The signs which had marked him as a boy had been put aside, the sacrifice was ended, and Marcus stood with flushed face and sparkling eyes, ready to be clothed with the toga, the emblem of manhood and citizenship. He drew a deep breath, as his father draped its graceful folds across his strong, young shoulders.

Lucius was almost as eager as Marcus, and as he looked at the brother whom he admired so much, he said to himself, "Marcus is no longer a boy; he is a man: a citizen of our great Roman Republic."

Then Marcus and Gaius, and all the members of the family, with the relatives and friends, and all the slaves of the household, formed in procession. It was a gay and happy procession, and a very large one as well.

They left the home of Gaius and made their way through the streets of the city to the great Forum. Here Marcus' name was entered in the public records as a citizen of the Republic, and then the friends and relatives crowded about him and offered him their best wishes, while Marcus—feeling very much like a boy, yet—smiled and blushed, and was very happy indeed.

But this was not the end of the ceremonies. The pro-

Marcus Stood With Flushed Face And Sparkling Eyes, Ready To Be Clothed With The Toga.

cession formed in order once more, and from the Forum they went up to the temple of Liber—from which we get our word "liberty." The temple was built upon one of the seven famous hills of Rome. Here an offering was laid upon the altar, and then the procession turned back toward the home of Gaius.

The day closed with a splendid feast.

"How fine Marcus looks in his toga," said Terentia to Lucius, during the feast.

"Yes," answered Lucius, but he said it with a sigh, for never before had he envied Marcus as he had on this day.

"And Tullius looks fine in his toga, too," Lucius added, for Tullius had put on the toga of manhood a month before.

Terentia blushed brightly at Lucius' speech, and Lucius suddenly asked, "When are you and Tullius to be married, Terentia?"

"In another month, little brother," Terentia replied with a happy smile.

After all the processions, the sacrifices, and the feasting of the day were over, the family was left alone in the big atrium. Marcus looked about him with a heart full of happiness and contentment. Gaius stood near the family altar, Gaia sat near him holding Livia in her lap, for the little girl was tired after all the excitement of the day. Terentia and Lucius stood by the fountain.

"Only one thing remains," said Marcus, "to make this the happiest day of my life."

Gaius smiled, for he understood what Marcus meant. He spoke to one of the slaves, and a moment later Glaucon entered the room.

Then Marcus stood erect, and looking very tall and manly, he turned to his faithful pedagogue and said: "Glaucon, I have been so very happy to-day, that I want to give a lasting happiness to some one else. My father has granted my wish, and shares it. To-morrow prepare yourself to go with us to the Forum, and there you shall receive what you well deserve to have—the gift of freedom." It was several moments before Glaucon could trust himself to speak. Then he said, with grave dignity, "The gift shows the heart of Marcus—a citizen of whom Rome may well be proud."

THE END.

www.ingramcontent.com/pod-product-compliance
Lightning Source LLC
Chambersburg PA
CBHW021337060726
47591CB00006B/2068